The Fruits Group

BY ANNABELLE TOMETICH

The Child's World®

Published by The Child's World®
1980 Lookout Drive • Mankato, MN 56003-1705
800-599-READ • www.childsworld.com

Acknowledgments
The Child's World®: Mary Berendes, Publishing Director
Red Line Editorial: Editorial direction
The Design Lab: Design
Amnet: Production
Photographs ©: Front cover: BrandX Images; FoodIcons; BrandX Images,
3, 4, 5, 7, 8, 9, 10, 13, 15, 16, 18; choosemyplate.gov, 5; FoodIcons, 6,
14, 23; GeneralFoodImages, 7; ComStock, 11, 12; Andresr/Shutterstock
Images, 19; Mediamix photo/Shutterstock Images, 21

ISBN: 978-1623236038
LCCN: 2013931393

Printed in the United States of America
Mankato, MN
July, 2013
PA02178

ABOUT THE AUTHOR

Annabelle Tometich writes about food and restaurants for The News-Press, a newspaper and multimedia company in Fort Myers, Florida. During her time as a sportswriter for The News-Press, Annabelle won three awards from the Associated Press Sports Editors. She lives in Fort Myers with her husband and young son.

Table of Contents

CHAPTER ONE

Sweet *and* Healthy

Fruits are sometimes called nature's candy. They are the parts of plants that carry seeds. Fruits grow from the ground, like strawberries, or on trees, like apples. Fruits are usually sweet thanks to their natural sugars. But unlike other sugary treats, fruits are filled with heart-healthy **vitamins**, **minerals**, and **fiber**. These help build strong bones and muscles. Eating plenty of fruits can help you run faster, skateboard farther, and jump higher.

▲ Fruits like apples and strawberries are sweet and healthy snacks.

▶ Opposite page: Use the MyPlate diagram to make healthy eating choices.

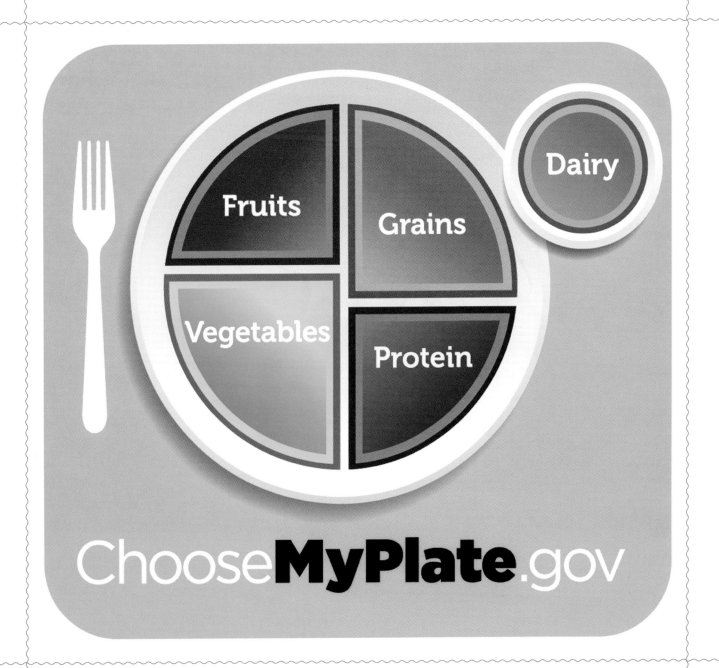

Fruits

Grains

Dairy

Vegetables

Protein

ChooseMyPlate.gov

The MyPlate diagram shows the five food groups that make up a healthy diet. The five groups are protein, grains, vegetables, dairy, and fruit. The diagram illustrates what your plate, bowl, or cup should look like at every meal. Fruits should take up about a quarter of your plate.

◄ Cherries are sweet and good for you.

▶ Raisins count as fruit in the MyPlate guidelines.

The MyPlate guidelines also count 100 percent fruit juices as servings of fruit. Juices such as orange juice and apple juice are squeezed from natural fruits. Dried fruits like raisins and prunes are also counted as fruits under the MyPlate guidelines. Fruits in cocktail cups count, too. But they count only if they are packed in fruit juice and not sugary syrups.

Fruits can be sweet *and* good for you. Fruits are important to a healthy diet no matter how you eat them. And a healthy diet is important to a healthy you.

CHAPTER TWO

How an Apple Helps You Grow

Fruits are filled with vitamins, minerals, and fiber. The next time you eat a banana, imagine your stomach breaking down each bite into tiny building blocks. These blocks are so small you cannot even see them with a magnifying glass.

These itty-bitty building blocks are called vitamins and minerals. They enter your blood after you eat healthy foods such as fruits. Your blood carries them

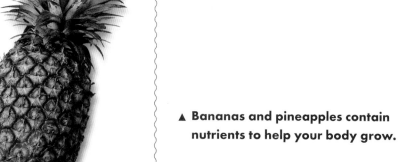

▲ Bananas and pineapples contain nutrients to help your body grow.

throughout your body. It delivers them to your brain, heart, lungs, bones, and muscles. The vitamin and mineral building blocks help make these parts of your body grow and become stronger. They also keep you from getting sick.

Dried apricots and cantaloupe have lots of vitamin A. Vitamin A helps you see better and makes your hair shiny and your skin healthy. When you slurp down a juicy slice of cantaloupe, you are eating the vitamin A building blocks it contains. You are helping your eyes, skin, and hair get the **nutrients** they need to be healthy.

Apples and lemons are full of magnesium. Magnesium is a mineral that keeps your heart

▶ Grapefruits are full of vitamin C.

◄ Fruits like strawberries have vitamin C that helps cuts heal.

healthy and your bones strong and sturdy. Strawberries, pineapple, and citrus fruits like oranges and grapefruits are high in vitamin C. Vitamin C helps cuts heal.

Fruits also have a lot of fiber. Fiber is the part of the fruit that your stomach cannot break down.

IN ONE END, OUT THE OTHER
Your body uses its digestive tract to break down food for nourishment. It starts with your mouth. Here, your teeth and saliva work to crush food into smaller pieces. When you swallow, the chewed-up food passes through a tube called the esophagus into your stomach. Then, it travels from your stomach to your small intestine. Next, it travels to the large intestine. Unused bits of food end up as bowel movements. Then the cycle starts over again.

▶ Fruits help keep your body strong and healthy.

Fiber plays an important role in helping you grow. It keeps your heart healthy and makes you feel full longer.

Fiber keeps things moving in your **digestive tract**. It helps move food from your stomach through your **intestines**. Fiber helps you have healthy, regular **bowel** movements, too. Regular bowel movements are just as important to your health as strong muscles and good vision.

Follow the MyPlate diagram and cover a quarter of your plate in fruit. Then you can be sure your body is getting all the building blocks it needs.

CHAPTER THREE

Counting Cranberries

MyPlate shows that kids ages four to eight should eat 1 to 1 1/2 cups of fruit every day. If you run around a lot, dance, or play sports, you should eat even more fruit to help power all your activities. A 1-cup serving is about the same size as a baseball. Ask an adult to curl one hand into a fist. This fist is also about the same size as 1 cup of fruit.

An apple that is 2 1/2 inches (6.5 cm) across counts as 1 cup of fruit. So does:

- One medium grapefruit
- 32 seedless grapes

▲ Fruit helps fuel your activities, like dancing.

▶ Opposite page: Chomp on some apple slices for a healthy snack.

- Three medium plums
- One small wedge of watermelon
- 1 cup orange juice

Dried fruits like raisins, prunes, and dried cranberries count double. This means a half a cup of raisins counts as 1 cup of fruit. Why? Raisins are grapes that have had the water inside them removed. Even though the water is gone, the grape's fibers and some nutrients are left behind.

By eating at least 1/3 cup of fruit with meals, you will reach your goal of one cup of fruit for the day. If your goal is 1 1/2 cups of fruit per day, then you need to eat at least 1/2 cup of fruit at each meal.

Measuring cups are tools you can use to figure out exactly how much fruit you are eating. At meals, you can fill a measuring

▼ Grab a bunch of grapes, an orange, or an apple for a serving of fruit.

▶ A half cup of blueberries count as a fruit serving.

THE WELL-NAMED WATERMELON

Did you know a watermelon is 92 percent water? The juicy fruit got its name for a reason. Early explorers used watermelons as a way to get water during long treks into unmapped areas. According to Guinness World Records, the world's heaviest watermelon was grown in Arkansas in 2005. It weighed 268.8 pounds. That's 247 pounds of water!

cup to the 1/3- or 1/2-cup line with strawberries or blueberries. Doing this will make sure you are eating exactly the amount of fruit you need. If a fruit is too big to fit into the measuring cup, have an adult cut it into pieces. This method will make it easier to measure. When you know exactly how much fruit you are eating, you know your body is getting the nutrients it needs to keep healthy.

CHAPTER FOUR

Chomp More Cherries

You have learned fruits are packed with things that help you grow strong and healthy. You have also learned that you need to eat 1 to 1 1/2 cups of fruit every day.

So how can you reach that goal? Next time your parents take you to the grocery store, walk through the produce section with them. That is the part of the supermarket where all of those colorful fruits and vegetables are kept. Instead of sugary treats, pick out your favorite fruits to take home.

Fruits taste best when they are **ripe**. Have you ever eaten a green banana? It was probably

▲ You can find cherries in your grocery store's produce section.

▼ Oranges and other citrus fruits have a lot of acid.

hard to bite and tasted bitter. As fruits ripen, their **starches** break down into a natural sugar called **glucose**. Glucose makes fruits taste sweet.

Unripe fruits have a lot of **acid**, like the acids that make lemons and limes sour. Acids make other fruits taste tart and bitter. As fruits ripen, acids disappear so you can taste their natural sugars.

Once you have ripe fruits in your house, all you have to do is eat them. You can enjoy them as they are or follow some of these suggestions:

Breakfast: Add slices of banana, blueberries, or strawberries to your cereal. Layer melon balls, dried fruits, or crushed pineapple from a can with yogurt. You will have a fruity breakfast parfait.

Lunch: Add apple slices to your peanut butter sandwich for a healthy crunch. Spread peanut butter onto a celery or carrot stick. Then top it with sweet raisins for a healthy side dish.

Dinner: Mix berries into salads for added sweetness. Make a fruit salsa out of mangoes, red peppers, and fresh herbs. Serve it with grilled chicken or fish.

Snacks: Take all your favorite fruits and mix them into a big fruit salad. Cover it and put it in the fridge for a healthy anytime snack.

Desserts: Top a scoop of frozen yogurt with banana slices, berries, pineapple, or dried cranberries to make a healthy sundae. Drizzle strawberries in a little bit of chocolate sauce or low-fat whipped cream.

Fruits are delicious any time of day. Just like proteins, vegetables, grains, and dairy, fruits are a key part of the MyPlate guidelines. When you eat

▼ Raspberries are great additions to your dinner salad.

EAT FRUIT, LIVE LONGER

Eating fruit each day may help you live longer. Scientists in the United Kingdom followed 11,000 healthy eaters for 17 years to see if what they ate affected their lives. The scientists found that people who ate the most servings of fruit daily lived longer. They had a much lower risk of heart disease and stroke than those who ate just one or two servings of fruit each day.

▶ Build a healthy body with fruits from your grocery store's produce section.

plenty of fruits you are building a healthy plate and a healthy body, too.

Hands-on Activity: Fruit Kabobs

These easy-to-make kabobs can be eaten as a side dish with any meal. They make a great anytime snack, too.

What You'll Need:

Wooden or metal kabob sticks, three types of firm fruits, like watermelon, grapes, bananas, cantaloupe, peaches, apples, or pineapples

Directions:

1. First, with an adult's help, cut each fruit into bite-sized pieces that are about the same size.
2. Next, hold the stick in one hand with its pointed end facing up. Pass the pointed end through the center of the first piece of fruit. Make sure the fruit is securely on the stick. Push the fruit down the stick, being careful not to poke your hand.

3. Then, pick a second, different piece of fruit. Pass the stick through it until the second piece is layered next to the first piece. Repeat for the third type of fruit. Then, start the pattern again with the first type of fruit. Continue layering your fruits until the skewer is full.

4. Enjoy your fruit kabobs immediately or cover them and refrigerate them for a snack for later.

Glossary

acid (AS-id): Acids are chemicals that usually have a sour taste. They are naturally found in fruits like lemons and limes.

bowel (BOW-uhl): Bowel is another word for your intestines, which are where digested food travels to after leaving your stomach. The bowel is part of the digestive tract.

digestive tract (dye-JESS-tiv trakt): The digestive tract is a series of tubes that pass food through your body after you eat it. The digestive tract breaks food down into minerals and vitamins your body can use.

esophagus (e-SAW-fuh-gus): The esophagus is the tube that connects a human's mouth and his or her stomach. The esophagus is part of the digestive system.

fiber (FYE-bur): Fiber is a substance found in plants such as fruits and vegetables. Fiber is the part of the fruit your body cannot break down.

glucose (GLOO-cose): Glucose is a type of sugar found in many kinds of fruits. Glucose gives fruit its sweet taste.

intestines (in-TES-tinz): The intestines are long tubes in a person's body that digest food after it leaves his or her stomach. Humans have large intestines and small intestines.

minerals (min-er-uhlz): Minerals are elements—such as calcium, magnesium, and iron—that are needed for the body to function and are found in food. People can get many of their daily minerals from fruits.

nutrients (NOO-tree-ents): Nutrients are substances that feed or nourish a body. Fruits contain lots of nutrients.

ripe (rype): Ripe means having achieved peak development. A ripe fruit is ready for eating.

starch (starch): Starch is the white, tasteless part of fruits and grains. Starches break down into glucose.

vitamins (VYE-tuh-minz): A vitamin is a substance found in foods that our bodies need to function properly. Fruits are a good source of vitamins.

To Learn More

BOOKS

Ely, Leanne. *Healthy Foods: An Irreverent Guide to Family Nutrition & Feeding Your Family Well.*
Fox Point, WI: Champion Press, 2001.

Taste of Home Kid-Approved Cookbook. Greendale, WI: Taste of Home Books, 2012.

WEB SITES

Visit our Web site for links about fruits: **childsworld.com/links**

Note to Parents, Teachers, and Librarians: We routinely verify our Web links to make sure they are safe and active sites. So encourage your readers to check them out!

Index